SWEET PERFECTION

KAT COLE

DISCLAIMER
THIS BOOK IS A NOVELETTE WHICH MEANS IT'S A LOT SHORTER THAN A NOVEL. IF YOU DON'T LIKE SHORT BOOKS, THEN THIS ISN'T THE BOOK FOR YOU. THIS IS THE INTRODUCTION TO THE MILLER SISTERS AND THE NEXT BOOK IN THIS SERIES WILL BE A FULL-LENGTH NOVEL.

I HOPE YOU ENJOY IT!
-KAT

DAZI

§

Save the date.

Save the date?

Did I seriously receive a wedding invitation from my ex-boyfriend? The same boyfriend I couldn't get to commit to me? The same boyfriend that treated me like a second option? The same boyfriend that didn't give a damn about my feelings and did whatever the hell he wanted?

Yeah.

It was him.

The nerve of this bastard.

I scoffed as I slowly walked up the driveway and through the front door so I could get a better look at the invite.

It was simple. There was a light pink heart at the top, and inside it had the words 'Save the Date'. Moving down just a little, it read:

Dania Marcus and Cain Harris are getting married!
SATURDAY, MAY 18TH, 2019

ATLANTA, GEORGIA

As I kept reading, I saw the address and rolled my eyes to the ceiling. It wasn't the address that made me roll my eyes. It was the entire thing.

Whenever I tried talking about marriage to Cain, it wouldn't do anything but start an argument. I couldn't understand it. How was he getting married already? It hadn't even been a full year since we officially broke up.

"Wow." I laughed bitterly while tossing all the mail on the small coffee table. I pushed out an annoyed breath then grabbed my phone to call my best friend Jazlyn. Maybe she would make me feel better about the situation.

The phone rang about four times before she picked up.

"Hello?" she sang.

"This nigga is getting married, Jaz. He sent me a fucking wedding invitation."

"Who?"

"Cain! We haven't even been broken up a full year, and he's already found a bitch to marry? That boy would damn near throw up whenever I brought up marriage. Like, what the fuck?"

"I know, Dazi. I got the invitation months ago."

My eyes went wide. "What? What the hell you mean months ago? Why didn't you tell me?"

"Because I didn't think it would last… I mean, you two had broken up not even a full threes months when I got the invitation. I honestly—"

"Wow. So, that means he was with her while we were still together. Niggas really ain't shit."

"You're right," she agreed. "But fuck him. We're not going to that wedding, and you're not gonna have to see him ever again."

"Oh, I'm going to that damn wedding. He clearly wants me to be there. Otherwise, he wouldn't have sent me this shit."

She sighed into the phone. "Don't do this. Going to that wedding won't do anything other than make you upset. You're obviously not over him, so—"

"I'm over him. I was over him when I broke things off with him."

I understand that, but what's the point of going? It's not going to do anything but piss you off, and knowing you, Dazi, you'd probably try to ruin the wedding."

My mouth fell open for a second before I quickly snapped it shut.

"I'm not going to say anything. I'm going to go, sit there quietly, and see what his new bitch looks like. I probably won't even stay the entire time."

"You know I don't believe you, right? You couldn't even sit quietly in church. What the hell makes you think you're gonna be able to sit quiet during his wedding? It's not a good idea. I'm trying to tell you."

"Don't care. I'm going. I'm going to make sure I look better than his new bitch too. Gonna look—"

"Dazi," she groaned. "Please don't do this."

"Doing it. You can come and support me if you want, but if not, I really don't care. I know for a fact that one of my sisters will come with me if not both."

"This plan is getting worse and worse. If your sisters go with you, they're gonna be the one to start some shit and you know it. Just leave Cain in the past. He wasn't a good boyfriend, anyway. I told you to break up with him how many times? But, you didn't want to listen to me. Don't let him fuck with you inner peace, Dazi."

I rolled my eyes. "He's not. I'll be good. But, I'll call you back. I need to get to the mall and find something nice to wear."

I ended the call before she could respond because I knew she wouldn't do anything but try to talk me out of it.

Scrolling through my phone again, I stopped right on my older sister Faith's contact and clicked on it. Like I knew she would, she answered on the second ring.

"Heyyy," she sang into the phone. "What you doin'? You wanna go to the bar and get drunk?"

Hell yes.

"Can't right now. I need you to come to the mall with me. I have to find an outfit for a wedding."

"A wedding? Who's getting married? Oh my God, you know how I feel about weddings. Can I be your plus one, please?"

"Of course you can. I'll be over in ten minutes. Be ready."

I didn't give her a chance to say anything else as I ended the call then walked into my room to put my shoes on.

After that, I made my way to the bathroom and quickly checked my appearance,

Satisfied with how I looked, I moved towards the front door and out the house, locking the door behind me.

I wasn't even a little shocked that Faith was excited about going. She had found a love for weddings when we were younger. Her feelings would probably change once she found out it was Cain's we were going to, but I didn't care. I was going to that wedding even if I had to go by myself.

Honestly, I couldn't wait to see what Cain's soon-to-be wife looked like. I already knew I looked better, and I was damn sure going to let it be known with the outfit I had planned.

Once I arrived at Faith's apartment, I found a close parking spot, then jumped out. I could've easily called her, but I felt like walking.

Lifting my hand to knock, I waited for about ten seconds before the door opened, and there stood Serenity, our oldest sister, looking like she belonged in a magazine.

"Hey, Dazi," she said as she crossed her arms. "I have a bone to pick with you."

"With me? What did I do?"

"You invited Faith to be your plus one and didn't even think to ask me, huh?"

"You're always too busy to hang out with us, so I just figured you would be busy."

She rolled her eyes. "Who do you even know that's getting married?"

I chewed the inside of my cheek while I debated if I wanted to tell her or not. She would feel the same way I felt about it, but she might be like Jazlyn and try to talk me out of it.

"Cain's. He's getting married. Next week, actually."

"What?" She twisted her face into a deep scowl as she flipped her platinum blond hair from her shoulder. "You're playing with me, right? Oh, you're not talking about the Cain you used to date."

"Nope. That's exactly who I'm talking about. He's getting married, and he sent me an invitation, so it's obvious that he wants me to be there."

She threw her head back with an obnoxious laugh. "What the hell? Why would you even want to go to that? It's not going to do anything but piss you off."

"It's not," I lied. "What is there to be pissed off about? He moved on. It's none of my business."

"Moved on? He was with her while y'all were together. There's no way he's getting married this quick and y'all haven't even been broken up that long. You'll probably be the one to stand up and object when they ask if anyone has something to say. It's a recipe for disaster."

"Anyway," I said, stepping past her and into the apartment. "Where's my nephew?"

"With his daddy. Where else would he be? You and your mom kill me with that. Whenever I don't have King, y'all ask where he is like I would just give him away to strangers."

Before I could respond, Faith was coming from the back with the biggest smile on her face.

"Hey," she said happily. "You got here way quicker than I thought."

"Hey Fai—"

"Faith, did you know that the wedding you're attending with your younger sister is Cain's?" Serenity just had to ask.

"Cain who?" Faith questioned with her face screwing up just like Serenity's did.

I pushed out an annoyed breath. "My ex Cain. We all only know one Cain. You know exactly who I'm talking about."

"Cain is getting married? To who? And you're going?"

"Yes, and yes. I have no idea who he's marrying, but I know he sent me an invite and I will be there looking good enough to eat. Are you ready to go to the mall or not? I'm not trying to be in there for too long."

Serenity smacked her lips. "Tell her it's a dumb ass idea to go to that wedding, Faith. You know it will end badly."

"It might not. He wants her to be there. He wouldn't have sent her an invitation otherwise."

I smiled at Faith for being on my side, and it was obvious that Serenity didn't like the answer she had given her.

"He sent her an invitation to piss her off. He probably doesn't even think she's going to show up, which she shouldn't. If your ex that you constantly brought up marriage to but told you he didn't want to get married sent you an invitation to his wedding, would you go?"

"I didn't constantly bring up marriage," I defended. "I said something about it maybe twice and he turned it down both times."

"Either way," Serenity cut in. "It's stupid that you even want to go. It's even stupider that you're about to go find an outfit for the wedding. Why won't y'all listen to me?"

"Because I'm going regardless," I chuckled. "Let's go, Faith." I started walking back towards the door and Faith grabbed her purse from off the counter.

"Well, when your little plan backfires, I don't want to hear anything about it. Don't come crying to me—"

"When do I ever come crying to you? Like I said, you're never around so you miss out on a lot of things."

"You're right about that one. I know you're a mom now, and you have a busy life, but dang. You could at least try to make time for your sisters. And one more thing. It doesn't matter what Dazi is trying to do. You should be there to support her one hundred percent because she's your sister. If we don't support her decisions, then who will?"

Serenity had a look of disgust on her face as I walked past her and out the door with Faith following right behind me.

"Well, whatever. You two have fun at the wedding. Something you probably won't be having no time soon because you're still doing things like this." She closed the door before I could respond to her and Faith grabbed my arm to keep me from going back in the apartment.

"Just ignore her, Dazi. You know how she is."

"I don't give a damn about any of that. She's always running her damn mouth, and one day, she's gonna get punched in it."

Faith didn't respond because she knew I was serious. She didn't like being in the middle of me and

Serenity's problems, but it never worked. She always got dragged in whatever me and Serenity had going on.

"But anyway, why didn't you tell me it was Cain's wedding we're going to? I can't believe he's even getting married," She said, once we made it to the car.

"I can't believe it, either. He literally told me he never planned on getting married, but here we are. Then, he had the nerve to send me an invitation? What if I go to this wedding and show my ass? Then what? He's gonna be doing a lot of regretting."

"You're not gonna show your ass, though. I'm not gonna let you." She gave me a small smile, then got in the passenger side of my car.

I didn't plan to act out when I got to the wedding, but I didn't know what might happen.

"I'm going to object when they ask—"

"No, the hell you aren't," she popped. "Why the hell would you do that? Do you want Cain? You want to be with him again?"

"No, but his wife needs to know that—"

"She doesn't need to know anything. If he treated you like shit and cheated, what makes you think he's not going to do the same thing to her? It's fine, Dazi. I know you're mad, but we're just gonna go to this wedding, you're gonna show him how good you look and how you're not even a little bitter over the fact that he's getting married, and that's the end of it. Nothing more, nothing less."

I rolled my eyes. "I am a little bitter, though."

"Don't be. Cain wasn't even that cute when you really looked at him. You can do better, and you will. Are you gonna let me do your makeup? And how the hell are you wearing your hair? When is the wedding?"

"Next weekend. I have no idea how I'm wearing my hair. I didn't think that far, yet. I just need to get an outfit."

She smiled at me again. "Well, I'm definitely doing your hair, too. I'm so excited. This wedding is going to be so fun."

Was it?

KAMARI

§

"It's a wedding, Kamari," my cousin Aaliyah said, twisting her face up. "Why do you have your grill in?"

"Why you always got something to say to me? Why can't you just stand over there and mind your business for once?"

"I'm trying to mind my business, but while everyone is looking nice and sophisticated, you're over there looking like a hood nigga. It shouldn't look like you're about to shoot a music video."

"I might be. Shit, you don't know what I have planned after this bullshit is over."

"Bullshit?!" she flipped. "My brother, who is your cousin is getting married. This is not bullshit. What's wrong with you?"

"I know how families work, Aaliyah. What the hell you even doin' over here? You're supposed to be over there with the girls, right?"

She smacked her lips. "I don't know his fiancé. I don't know why she even asked me to be a bridesmaid."

"You do know her," Cain said, coming out the bathroom. "Y'all know each other enough when she wants to talk shit about me all night on the damn phone."

"Having phone conversations and being in someone's wedding are so different. I told you—"

"Go check on Dania, please."

She muttered something under her breath, then left out the room completely.

Cain admired himself in the full-length mirror, then let out a small laugh.

"I should've gotten married sooner if I knew I was gonna look this good in a tux," he said, dead ass serious.

"Nigga, I can't believe you're getting married. Dania finally talked you into the shit, huh?"

He turned to look at me. "Nah, she didn't. I had told her I didn't see myself getting married, and she left it alone, but then I started thinking. Me and her have been together for a little minute now and it felt like the right thing to do. I wouldn't want six years to just go to waste, so I decided it's time to give her my last name, and maybe a few babies."

"I mean, I'm just a little shocked because the last time I saw you, weren't you serious with someone else? You know I'm bad with names."

"Dazi? We weren't even supposed to fuck around for as long as we did. She was just hella addictive. It's actually hard to explain, but Dania went through my phone more than once and caught me talking to Dazi. Couldn't have that shit keep happening, then Dania decides she doesn't want my ass anymore, so I cut Dazi off. She was just a side chick, anyway."

"Damn, so you never wanted her? Y'all looked pretty serious to me."

He shook his head. "Hell naw. Then, she liked to bring up marriage and shit, not even knowing I basically already had a wife. Dazi was only good to fuck and nothing else. She got annoying quick as fuck."

"So," I lifted a brow. "If I ran into her on the streets or something, you wouldn't get mad if I—"

"Nah. You can have her."

The door flew open, and in walked an angry Aaliyah.

"What the fuck, Cain? Why did you invite Dazi? Do you want today to turn to shit?" she snapped, standing in front of him while crossing her arms.

"I didn't invite her. You and Dania were in charge of the invites. Y'all did this shit."

"Oh my God," she pushed out. "Why would she even come? I know y'all didn't end on good enough terms for her to be okay with watching you get married to someone that's not her. Then, her outfit. She has on a white, tight ass dress, and her hair is like a bright green color. She clearly wants all the attention to be on her. I think I'm going to ask her to leave."

"What? Man, hell nah. That wouldn't do anything but cause more problems. She'll really cause a scene if you try to put her out, so just let her sit there. Don't even look in her direction. Act like she's not here."

"I already looked at her… and she waved at me."

"Well, don't look at her anymore, Aaliyah, shit."

I could see the instant change in his demeanor, which was a little funny to me.

"You think Dania knows who she is? I mean, that's the only way I can think she even got an invitation because I know for a fact I didn't send her one."

Cain pinched the bridge of his nose. "I don't know, Aaliyah. This ain't the shit I'm tryna be talking about on my wedding day. We'll discuss it later."

She screwed her face up. "Discuss it later? Why—"

"What the fuck did I just say?" He looked down at his watch and pushed out an aggravated breath. "It's time to start this shit. Go."

Aaliyah said nothing as she left the room again, and Cain shook his head.

"I feel like I talked the bitch up," he said in disbelief. "Ain't no reason she should be here. I feel like someone is playing a joke on my ass, bruh."

I laughed at his dumb ass. "Couldn't be me. But, it's time to do this shit. You wanna keep them mothafuckas out there waitin'?"

He sighed loudly, then walked out of the room with me following behind him. In the hallway, we met up with my older brother Saint, and he looked at me with his eyes red and low.

"Nigga, you look high as fuck," I laughed, causing Cain to glance at him. "How you gon' smoke and not invite me? That's fucked up."

"Man, I was trying to, but I couldn't find yo ass."

I smacked my lips. "Where did you look?"

"I glanced around when I was outside and on the way to my car." He let out a loud laugh.

"See, I always knew you weren't shit."

"Will y'all shut the fuck up?" Cain snapped, but Saint kept laughing.

"Damn, nigga. The fuck we do to you?"

"Y'all talkin' too damn much right now. I'm trying to focus."

"Cain, I know you stressin' because you got your side bitch at your wedding, but let that be the last time you tell me to shut the fuck up. You had a little too much bass in your voice, nigga."

He didn't respond, and that was his best bet. Cousin or not, I would beat his ass on his wedding day.

Cain opened the door, and we followed behind him where everyone was waiting for this bullshit wedding to start. Immediately, my eyes landed on Dazi who was busy glaring at Cain.

She damn sure stuck out like a sore thumb because of her lime-green hair, but not on no ghetto shit. She looked good. She was fine as hell with her bright hair long and bone straight flowing down her back, and she was sitting down, but I could see how the white strapless dress she had on made her body look delectable.

We took our spots upfront with Saint standing behind me, and on the other side were Dania's two bridesmaids. One of them kept staring me down like she knew she looked good enough for me to be interested, but she was sadly mistaken.

"Aye," Saint whispered from behind me. "Who is that with the green hair? She fine as fuck."

"That's Dazi. Cain was fucking her, and he doesn't know how she got an invite to the wedding."

"I'm not tryna keep starin', but I can see her nipples through her dress."

I quickly glanced back over to Dazi, and she flipped her hair from her shoulder, giving me full access to her hardened nipples.

I'm not the type that's gonna pass a girl up just because she was fucking with my cousin or homeboy. If she's down to fuck, then that's what I'm gonna do, and Cain had already given me the okay even though that shit didn't matter.

"Yeah. I'ma see what's up with her."

"Her friend is cute. Looks kinda stuck up, but I could probably get her to fuck."

We discreetly dapped each other up while letting out quiet laughs, then the music finally began to play.

The doors to the church opened, and Dania started walking down the aisle accompanied by her dad, and everyone stood up. I took this chance to look back at Dazi and admired how good her slim body looked in the dress.

I was happy for Cain that he was getting married and shit, but I was ready for this shit to be over with so I could approach Dazi before she left.

Cain didn't look happy to see Dania walking down the aisle, but she was all smiles. He really felt some type of way because his side chick was here, but Dazi was behaving. She was watching Dania walk down the aisle with a blank expression on her face.

Being that I didn't give a fuck about the talking part of the wedding, it felt like the shit took forever. I was happy as fuck when they finally kissed and everyone cheered for them. Everyone except Dazi.

While everyone stood to their feet and clapped, Dazi remained seated with her friend right next to her scrolling on her phone.

"You goin' to that reception shit?" Saint asked while everyone tried to make their way out of the church.

"Yeah, but I probably won't stay for long. I'ma go just to get some liquor."

"Aight. I'll just ride with you, then."

I didn't bother responding to him because I saw Dazi and her friend finally stand up, and I rushed over there before they could get out the door.

"What's up?" I questioned as Dazi turned around to look at me. "You're wearing the hell out of that dress, ma."

She let her eyes roam all over my body before locking eyes with me.

"I know that."

I smiled at her confidence. "You going to the reception?"

She shook her head. "Hell no. I don't think Cain would want me there. It's probably for the best I don't show up."

"For what? You got invited to the wedding, didn't you? He wouldn't have invited you if he didn't want you to come." Yeah, I was on bullshit, but I wanted to see Dazi at the reception.

Up close, she was even finer.

She had smooth brown skin, full lips, a silver hoop nose piercing, and a few tattoos were on each arm. It was hard for me to keep my attention on her face because her body was crazy. I was about to tell her to just come chill at my crib with me instead of going to this damn reception.

"Is there gonna be alcohol there?" she questioned, lifting a brow.

"Yeah. That's the only reason I'm going."

"Alright. I'll go. Where is it?"

"Follow behind me. I'll lead the way."

She stared at me saying nothing before she turned to walk out the church with her friend right next to her.

"But aye, we might need to exchange numbers just in case you get lost tryna follow me," I said, watching her turn her head in my direction.

"What?" She laughed. "Why don't you just give me the address then? Wouldn't that make more sense?"

"Nah," I shook my head. "I like my idea better. Plus, you look too good for me not to have your number."

Finally, a small smile crossed her face. "You think you cute, huh?"

"Think? Nah, I know that shit. All this time we're wasting from just standing here. I could've been had your number by now."

She lifted an amused eyebrow. "Who the hell said I wanted to give you my number? I don't even know your name. You think just because you complimented me on how good I look that I'm just supposed to give you my number? Is that how it usually works for you?"

"I don't know why you're playing. You know you're gonna give me your number, anyway." I chuckled lightly as I pulled my phone out, unlocked it, then handed it to her.

Her smile deepened, and she took my phone from me and quickly stored her number.

"So," she let out, running her fingers through her hair. "Are you going to tell me your name now, or not? You look hella familiar."

"Kamari."

"Okay, Kamari. I'm gonna follow behind you." We started walking out the church together, and I noticed her friend didn't say anything. She kept her face buried in her phone, but from what I could see, she was cute too. I was still more interested in Dazi, though.

"Did you find out her friend's name?" Saint asked once we were at my car.

"Nah. She didn't say shit. I'm not worried about her friend, though. You're gonna have to do that shit on your own, nigga."

He smacked his lips. "Don't say it like I'm not capable of getting my own bitches. I bet I'll have her ass at my crib bent over the couch before the night is over."

I let out a small laugh. "If you say so. She might have a boyfriend."

"Dazi might have a boyfriend, too. You didn't even think to ask, did you?"

"That's the difference between me and you, though. I'm not gonna give a fuck if she does have a boyfriend. She looks like she tastes like a red gummy bear, and I'm tryna find out."

He looked at me for a second before he threw his head back with a loud laugh. "It's something wrong with you, nigga. The clear gummy bears are better than the red ones, anyway."

"Get the fuck outta here. Ain't nothing better than the red ones. You trippin'." I pulled the door open and slid into the driver's seat, and he did the same.

I started the car, then drove up a few cars where Dazi was parked. Once I had her attention, I slowly pulled off, and she followed behind me, then we were on our way to the bullshit reception.

The fact that I talked Dazi into coming had me excited. I didn't plan to stay at the reception long, but there was no telling what might happen now that I had someone to keep me occupied.

DAZI

§

"Did you see how Cain was looking at me?" I chuckled, following close behind Kamari. "He looked like he didn't want me to be there, but sent me an invitation?"

"He was probably mad at how good you look," Faith beamed, running her fingers through my hair. "Aren't you glad I talked you into wearing this wig? It looks so good against your skin. People paid more attention to you than they did the actual bride."

"The bride didn't look like anything. I don't know where Cain found her ass, but he didn't even look happy as she walked down the aisle."

I wouldn't say she was ugly... she just didn't have shit on me. The wedding ceremony could've been a lot better, too, but that was none of my business.

"Kamari is cute," she said, causing me to glance in her direction. "Tall, light-skinned, nice lips. You obviously got his attention."

"Yeah, I guess he is cute."

Cute?

Cute?

No, that definitely wasn't the word to describe him. The first thing I noticed about him was his height. He towered over me, which I loved. I didn't need a short man trying to talk to me because that wouldn't lead to anything but me hurting his feelings.

His full, pink lips were what I noticed next. They looked pillow-soft, and I didn't feel bad when I envisioned his set of lips on my other set of lips. His mustache was perfect, and from the looks of it, his beard was still coming in, but it wasn't patchy. His hair was cut, but his waves were on point. I honestly don't think I'd ever seen anyone with waves that looked as good as his.

His eyes were hazel. When I noticed it, I wanted to take my panties off and throw them at him right then and there, and then when he smiled at me? Showing me the gold he had on his bottom row of teeth? That was it for me.

I acted like I didn't want to give him my number, but on the inside, I was jumping for joy.

"You guess he's cute?" Faith laughed. "Girl, when he approached you, your mouth damn near fell open. You know that man is fine. You should bust it wide open for him."

"Oh, my God. I'm not going to bust it—"

"Yes, you are. If you don't plan to, why are we going to the reception? That wasn't part of the plan. You said you didn't want to watch them have their first dance or give speeches. But then fine ass Kamari came about and here we are."

I smiled to myself. "We're not staying long. I'm going to get a few drinks, talk to Kamari, then I'm leaving."

"Mhm," She giggled. "You gonna talk to Kamari with your vagina?"

"What? I don't even know him. I'm not thinking about sex—"

"Shut the hell up. You know that's the only thing you're thinking about. I'm happy for you, though. Show up to your ex's wedding and leave with the finest nigga there. You've always been like that, though. Niggas just be fallin' at your feet."

I rolled my eyes. "No the hell they don't."

"They do. I scanned the entire building for cute niggas and there were only two. Kamari and the big dude standing next to him. I bet you didn't even notice Kamari while he was up there, did you?"

"Nope," I shook my head. "I was too busy watching Cain watch me. Had his whole wife in front of him, but couldn't keep his eyes off me."

Faith smacked her lips. "Girl, please shut the hell up about Cain. Cain doesn't matter anymore. Cain is irrelevant now because he has a wife. Cain doesn't look as good as Kamari. He's who you need to be thinking about. You saw just like I saw how good that man looked in that tux. Just delicious. Please have sex with him soon, then tell me how it was. Pleaseeee."

"Or, you could have sex with him and tell me how it was."

She cut her eyes in my direction, but I kept my eyes on the road.

"Dazi, shut the hell up. You know damn well if I try to do anything with him, you're gonna feel some type of way. Why are you trying to downplay it like you're not interested in him?"

"I'm not trying to downplay anything."

"Yeah, okay."

It didn't take us long to arrive at the building the reception was being held at, and to my surprise, it was nice.

I'm not saying that I expected it to be at a rundown building, but I also knew Cain, and he would've never done something like this for me.

"Wow," I scoffed. "I can't believe this nigga. You should've seen the way he reacted whenever I brought up marriage."

"Because he didn't want to marry you. I know you probably don't wanna hear this, but I wouldn't be me if I didn't keep it real with you. Y'all were broken up for what, six months, and here he is getting married to someone else. They couldn't have been together for that long and there's already a wedding. An exact representation of niggas will act right for the one they really wanna be with."

She was right. I didn't want to hear that shit.

I decided not to respond to her because I would only take my anger out on her, then I parked a few cars down from Kamari.

"Definitely not staying long," I muttered, flipping my hair from my shoulder.

I checked my appearance in the mirror before I popped my door open and stepped out, and Faith did the same thing.

Kamari casually walked to my car and eyed my body with a look of pure lust in his eyes, then turned his attention to Faith.

"My bad, shorty, I didn't get your name."

Faith looked up at him. "Because I didn't offer it."

He laughed lightly. "Y'all sisters?"

I nodded. "Yep. This is my older sister Faith. I don't know why she's acting like that."

Some guy came to stand next to Kamari and let his attention fall on Faith.

"What's your name, ma?" he questioned while blowing out smoke from the blunt he was smoking.

"Not interested. Can we go in here now? There's no reason to still be standing outside."

Faith led the way, and Kamari laughed at how she'd just blown his friend off.

Just like the outside of the building, the inside looked just as good.

I was so wrapped up looking around at the decorations, I didn't even see Cain approaching me with the ugliest expression on his face.

"What the fuck are you doing here, Dazi?" he spat, causing my face to instantly frown.

"Nigga, you sent me an invitation—"

"I didn't send yo' ass shit! I told you I was done with you, right? What the fuck makes you think I would want you here? Leave! I had to look at you during the ceremony, but I'm damn sure not about to—"

"Chill the fuck out, bruh. She's here with me. She ain't goin' nowhere," Kamari said easily.

"The fuck you just say?" Cain questioned, taking a step closer to him like he was ready to do something.

"You heard what the fuck I said, nigga. You out of all people know how I feel about repeating myself. I don't know who the fuck you steppin' to, either. Don't get embarrassed in here."

Cain just glared at Kamari, then turned his attention back to me. I smiled at him, knowing it only pissed him off even more, and we all walked away and found a table to sit at.

"Oh wow," Faith whispered to me. "He must really want the pussy if he's taking up for you like that."

"Shut up," I laughed, watching Kamari pull out a chair for me. "Thank you," I said sitting down.

He was a gentleman, too?

His friend did the same for Faith, and she just plopped down without saying a word to him.

"I'm Saint, by the way," he said, sitting down next to Faith. "You gonna let me know what your name is now?"

She smiled at him. "I will as soon as you buy me a drink."

He raised a brow. "What? That's all you want?"

"Yep."

Saint quickly left the table and made his way over to the bar.

I could feel eyes on me, so I glanced up, and Cain was sitting next to his wife, but staring at me with nothing but murder in his eyes.

It made me feel good knowing that I had him that bothered, but my question was, why did he invite me if he didn't want me to be here?

"How do you know Cain?" I asked Kamari. "I mean, y'all must be close for him to have you in his wedding."

"We're cousins."

Cousins?

"Oh," I said, hoping he couldn't hear the defeat in my voice. "You know I dated him, right?"

He let out a sexy chuckle. "Yeah, I know. He brought you around me once or twice."

"He did?" I knew Kamari looked familiar, but I had no idea we'd met through Cain before.

"Yeah. You were probably too far up his ass to notice a real nigga." Not once did he crack a smile. He was dead serious.

"That's crazy. I'm gonna get something to drink, though." I stood up, and he did the same.

"You think I'm about to let you buy your own drink?" He laughed. "You're funny as hell."

He began making his way to the bar, and I followed. Saint was walking back towards the table with Faith's drink in his hand.

Saint wasn't ugly. His skin was damn near the same color as Kamari's, he was taller, and from the looks of it, he had more muscles on him too. He had full pink lips just like Kamari, and honestly, they kinda resembled.

"Are you and Saint related, too?"

"Yeah. He's my brother."

"Oh wow," I looked over at the table and he was all in Faith's face. From the looks of it, she wasn't trying to give him the time of day. "Is he older?"

"Yep. What you like drinkin' though? You look like you would like those fruity ass drinks."

I threw my head back with a light laugh. "Um, no. I want something dark. Maybe some Hennessy."

"Oh shit. You tryna get lit, huh?"

"Yep. Not trying to drink to be cute."

He gave me a small smirk before he stepped in front of me and ordered me some Hennessy, then Rum and Coke for himself.

After that, he handed me my cup with nothing but Hennessy in it, and I looked down at it. I expected it to either be shots, or maybe mixed with something, but it wasn't. It was straight Hennessy, and I swallowed hard.

Usually, I started to act up when I drank brown, but at this very moment, I didn't give a damn.

"Thank you for this," I said, taking a small sip. It burned going all the way down, but I kept a poker face so Kamari wouldn't think I was a lightweight.

Slowly, we walked back to our table where Saint was still trying to sweet talk Faith, but she wasn't having it. From the look she wore on her face, I could tell she wasn't interested, but I didn't understand why. I couldn't wait until we left so I could ask her why she wouldn't give Saint's fine ass the time of day.

"Damn, so you're not even gonna let me get your number? How am I gonna take you out if I can't get in contact with you?" he asked, invading her personal space.

"First off, back the hell up, nigga," She laughed. "Secondly, what makes you think I want to go to the movies with you? I don't know you, for one, and two," She put her drink down and stared directly into his eyes. "You're not my type."

Saint just smiled at her. What she said didn't even phase him.

"What's your type, ma?"

"I like small short niggas," she let him know. "Niggas that wear glasses. Oh, and I really love when they still live at home with their mom. That just puts the icing on the cake for me."

"What? You serious?"

"As a heart attack."

I chuckled lightly as I took a few more sips from my drink. Faith knew she was feeling Saint. I couldn't remember the last time she had had a man or someone she was just having sex with. For a long time, I thought she liked girls, but she always denied it.

"It has to be something wrong with you if you like bum ass niggas," he said, shaking his head. "That doesn't mean I'm gonna stop trying, though." Saint was so confident, and Faith waved him off.

I continued taking small sips of my drink, and slowly but surely, the affects took over.

"So," I slurred a little. "What do you do for a living, Kamari?" I gently placed my hand on his chest.

"You serious?"

My brows came together. "Yeah…"

"Like, you dead ass right now?"

"I wouldn't have asked if I already knew."

"That nigga a—"

"Nah," he said, cutting Saint off. "We're gonna let her figure that out on her own."

"What? Why can't you just tell me what you do for a living? It's something illegal, isn't it?"

He shook his head. "Nah. Not anymore. You'll figure it out sooner than later, though."

I rolled my eyes and decided to just let it go. I wasn't about to play twenty-one questions just to find out where he worked. It wasn't that serious.

By the time I finished my drink, I was good and drunk, and Cain was getting everyone's attention so he could say something.

"I guess it's time for me to make a speech, huh?" he said over the microphone. Everyone turned their attention to him, including me. "I wanna start off by saying thank you to everyone who came and supported Dani and I on our big day. Six years ago when we first started dating, I always knew she was the woman I wanted to marry." He smiled down at her, and my chest tightened.

Did he just say six years?

So… I was the side chick?

I glanced at Faith who was already looking at me, which let me know she heard the bullshit that came out of his mouth, too.

"I was the side chick," I chuckled out loud in disbelief.

"You didn't know?"

I looked at Kamari like he was crazy.

"No. This whole time, I thought me and him were in a real relationship. No wonder his mom didn't like me. I never did anything to the bitch, but she always had a problem when I came around."

"Damn, ma. How long did y'all fuck around?"

"Fuck around?" I flipped. "We were together for two years. Two whole years, but he was already in a committed relationship. Ain't that some shit?"

I knew coming to this damn reception was a bad idea. I should've just taken my ass home.

Kamari probably thought since I was a side bitch that I'd be an easy fuck.

I couldn't even hide the scowl on my face as the embarrassment set it.

Cain was still going on with his speech, but I wasn't listening to a damn thing he had to say. It wasn't like it mattered, anyway.

"What did Cain say about me? What made you approach me?" I knew I most likely wouldn't like the answer, but that wasn't what I was worried about.

"Earlier, he told me I could have you. I saw how good you looked and already knew what was up."

"What was up? So, you think I'm just going to have sex with you because I was a side chick? Is that what this is?"

His brows dipped together. "What?"

"You think I'm a hoe? You think I just barge my way into nigga's lives and make them cheat on their girlfriends? You think I'm a desperate bitch, don't you? Well, I'm not. Ain't nothing desperate about me," I jabbed a finger into my chest. "Nothing."

Without waiting for a response from him, I got up from the table and began to make my way to the bathroom. I caught the somber look that was on Faith's face, which did nothing but piss me off more than I already was.

Once I was in the bathroom, I blew out an annoyed breath, ignoring the woman who was already in there washing her hands.

"What's wrong, Dazi? You found out watching the nigga you can't have get married wasn't one of your best ideas?"

I turned my attention to her, not even surprised it was Aaliyah standing there looking like it satisfied her that I was clearly in a pissed off mood.

"I don't want your hoe ass brother," I laughed, which only caused her to laugh too.

"You don't? Then why the hell did you show up at his wedding? I know for a fact he said he would never marry you. Why would he want to marry someone who's okay with being in second? You really need to learn your worth, girl."

"Bitch, your brother was lying to me. He never said anything about having a girlfriend. He—"

"Girl, bye. I know he said something to you about Dania. I just hope you don't turn into one of those side bitches that doesn't know how to let go. You're too pretty for that."

I glared at her, and before I could respond, the door was opening, and in walked Kamari, holding his cup and looking good enough to eat.

"Get the fuck out, Aaliyah," he demanded, and she twisted her face up at him.

"Excuse me? This is the ladies' room. You're the one that shouldn't be in here." She folded her arms as Kamari moved towards me with his eyes never leaving mine.

"I didn't ask all that. I said get the fuck out. Not gonna say it again."

"I don't care about any of that. You must think I'm scared of you because you got everyone else scared of you, but—"

Kamari pulled his tuxedo jacket back just enough to show her the gun that was tucked in the waist of his pants, and it shut her right up.

"What were you saying?" he questioned, finally turning his attention to her.

The fear played out all over her face, but she was still trying to act like she wasn't scared.

"Whatever, Kamari. Don't know why you're so pressed to talk to a hoe, anyway." She quickly left the bathroom, and I ignored her comment.

Aaliyah and I both knew that if it ever came down to it, I would beat her ass with no questions asked.

"Look," Kamari said taking a step closer to me. "I don't give a fuck about none of the shit you just said. I approached you because that was some shit I wanted to do. Cain didn't have shit to do with it. Even if he wouldn't have told me I could have you, I still would've done the same shit because you look good as fuck, and I wanna know what you taste like."

I bit the inside of my cheek to suppress a smile. It made me feel a lot better to know he wasn't trying me because he thought I was desperate.

"From what I hear," I responded, flipping my hair from my shoulder. "I taste good as hell."

He flashed me a grin before he gently grabbed my chin with his large hand and roughly stuck his tongue in my mouth.

My heart rate sped up while I tasted the liquor on his tongue, and damn near moaned into his mouth from the way he gripped my ass with one hand.

"Get that ass on the sink," he demanded when he pulled away.

I looked in the sink's direction — which was nice as hell, then returned my attention back to him. He was moving towards the door to lock it.

"I know you heard what the fuck I said, Dazi." My name just rolled off his tongue and hit me right in the lady parts. He oozed sex appeal as he casually made his way back over to me with his bottom lip tucked in, and eyes low.

"I heard you. I want you to make me."

Usually, I wouldn't have sex with a random stranger that I had literally just met not even a full two hours ago, but as I said before, Hennessy made me act up.

Kamari smirked at me before he quickly lifted me up and sat me down on the counter.

"I hope you know what you're doing," I teased, watching him bring his cup to his lips. There wasn't anything in it but ice, and he put a few in his mouth, while never letting his eyes leave mine.

"Keep these legs open." He spread my legs as far as they would go, and I leaned back onto the mirror, not caring how cold it was on my back.

Kamari dipped his head low and put his mouth on me, causing me to let out a loud moan. His mouth was freezing cold from the ice, and I had no idea it would only intensify the feeling.

"Shit," I whimpered, feeling him swirling his tongue around along with the ice that had yet to melt. It was getting harder and harder to keep my legs open, but I was determined because I was running my mouth a little before he'd even started.

He dug his fingers into my thighs, keeping my legs open and my body shook gently against his mouth.

Hell no. There's no way I'm about to cum this quick from head.

Kamari had his face all in it. He was applying just enough pressure, and the feeling quickly became too much for me.

"Ohhhh!" My legs closed in on him and he brought his hazel eyes up to mine.

"What I tell you to do, girl?" he questioned, finally coming up for air. "I told you to keep them legs open, didn't I?"

I couldn't respond to him because he slid a thick finger inside me, poking spots I had no idea were even there.

"Shut up," I breathed, watching a sexy smirk spread across his lips. "What I taste like?"

He grabbed my face again and stuck his tongue in my mouth, and I tasted myself all over his lips.

"A red gummy bear," he muttered against my lips, causing me to smile.

"The best kind."

He curved his fingers just enough to make my body tremble, and I threw my head back in pure ecstasy.

I wasn't trying to muffle my moans, and I was sure if anyone was standing outside the door, they could hear everything that was going on.

"You hear how wet that shit is?" he questioned, letting his lips hover over my ear. "Who did that shit, ma?"

"You," I sighed, wrapping my arms around his neck, pulling him closer to me.

"Nah, what's my name?"

He slid another finger inside me, and the orgasm snuck up on me. "Kamari!"

He smiled at me, showing off his perfect teeth and the moans got stuck in my throat. There was no way he was making me cum back to back with only his fingers.

"Give me one more, baby," he demanded in a low voice. "One more."

My body easily submitted to him. Honestly, I could probably cum from just hearing his voice because as soon as the words left his lips, my body was trembling again, and I released my juices all over his fingers.

"There you go."

Slowly, he removed his fingers from inside me then pressed his lips against mine which turned into us tongue wrestling for about five minutes.

After that, he grabbed some paper towels, wet them, then cleaned me up like a gentleman.

"Thank you. You're so nice," I smiled, watching as he got himself together. "I wouldn't want you to go back out there with a wet pussy even though you got me hard as fuck right now."

I lifted a brow. "Why don't we—"

"I don't have any condoms on me. I didn't think I would be ready to fuck at my cousin's wedding."

Once he was finished with me, he helped me off the sink.

"So, you really don't care that I messed around with Cain?"

He chuckled lightly. "I just had my tongue all in your pussy and mouth. Does it look like I give a fuck about any of that?"

A smile crossed my face, and I stood there for a few seconds trying to get the feeling back in my legs.

He started walking towards the door, then turned around when he noticed I wasn't following him.

"What you doin'? Come on, girl."

"I can't really feel my legs yet."

He let out a small laugh and walked back over to me, grabbing my hand. After that, he slowly walked out the bathroom, and I tried my hardest not to smile as Cain's family stared at us.

I locked eyes with Cain, and his entire body tensed up. For the life of me, I couldn't understand why

Cain was feeling some kind of way when he was the one that told Kamari he could have me.

When we got back to the table, Faith's eyes fell on me, and it was damn near impossible not to smile at her. I wanted to act like nothing happened between me and Kamari, but it was obvious. Maybe a little too obvious.

*****

"So, you're gonna sit there and act like nothing happened?" Faith questioned once we were in the car.

"What are you talking about?"

"Don't play with me. You and Kamari disappeared for a long time. You left me at the table with Saint by my damn self. That nigga annoying as hell. Then, when y'all finally came back to the table, you couldn't stop smiling. What the fuck was that?"

I smiled again thinking about how good Kamari made my body feel.

"What's wrong with Saint? He seems sweet, and you're acting like you weren't even interested."

"Because I wasn't."

"Why not? He's cute, tall, and funny as hell. He—"

"He probably has a lot of hoes, and I'm not trying to be one of them. I can see that type of guy he is just from looking at him. That's not what I want to talk about, though. I want to talk about you and Kamari. Did you fuck him in the bathroom?"

I laughed lightly to myself. "No. I didn't fuck him in the bathroom. He fingered me a little… and ate me out."

"Dazi!"

"What? He wanted to do it, so I let him. You ever been eaten out with ice before? You know what that feels like? I'm shocked everyone didn't hear me in there. Swear to God I had an out-of-body experience."

"Him and Cain are cousins though. You don't think—"

"Nope," I said, cutting her off. "He didn't care, so why should I? Also, let Cain tell it, me and him were never together being that I was only the side chick. Two whole years, and I was the side? Fuck Cain. I got Kamari's number, too. I plan on putting this pussy on him real soon."

She shook her head. "I can't believe you. I mean, I'm happy for you, but at the same time, I just can't believe you."

"Well, believe it."

It didn't take long to get to Faith's apartment, and I rolled my eyes seeing Serenity's car in the parking lot.

"Why did you give that girl a key?" I questioned, pulling up right next to her car.

"I asked her to do something for me a long time ago while I was at work, and she never gave me the key back. She comes over here when Lamar is pissing her off, but she loves to put on a front like they're in the happiest relationship."

"Honestly, I don't even wanna see her. I'll call you later, okay?"

"Okay." She popped the door open and stepped out the car, and I quickly pulled off, heading toward my place.

My phone began ringing in the cup holder, and I looked down at it, seeing that it was an unknown number.

Against my better judgment, I swiped my finger across the screen and put the phone to my ear.

"Hello?"

"So, this is really the hoe shit you're on, Dazi?" Cain questioned, and I could feel the silent anger creeping up.

"What the fuck are you talking about, Cain? Wait, no, the better question is, why are you calling my phone with this bullshit? Does your wife know you're on the phone with your old side chick?"

"Don't worry about my wife, bruh!"

"And don't worry about who I'm fuckin', nigga!"

"I'm not worried about shit! I just want to know why you thought it was okay to fuck my cousin? At my fucking wedding!"

I threw my head back with a loud laugh. "First off, it wasn't at your wedding. It was at the reception. Get your facts straight. Secondly, you've been with that bitch for six years, so honestly, this conversation is pointless. You told Kamari he could have me right? You don't give a fuck about me right?"

"Man, fuck that! I don't give a fuck what I said. You have no right—"

"Boy, fuck you! What the fuck you mean I have no right? I am single. I can do what I want and who I want, and your cousin just happened to be feeling the same way I was feeling. Why the fuck would you invite me to your wedding if you didn't want me there? Huh?"

"That's the thing! I didn't invite yo' ass! I don't know how you got an invitation, but you were the last person I wanted to see! Today was supposed to be the happiest day of my life, and you know what you did? You fucking ruined it!"

"Good," I smiled. "I'm so glad I could do that."

"Fuck you, Dazi. You won't ever be good enough to be someone's wife. You'll always be side chick material. Fuckin' a nigga on the first day and you barely even know him? That's some top of the line hoe shit, bruh. I'm glad I was never in a serious relationship with you."

I didn't bother to respond and hung up on him. The conversation wasn't doing anything but pissing me off, and I didn't need that. Cain was a nobody. I should've never been dealing with him in the first place.

KAMARI

§

"What, Aaliyah? What the fuck you just standing right here in my way for?" I asked as Aaliyah stood in front of me with her arms folded.

"So, you just don't know what loyalty is, huh? You'll fuck any woman who looks at you?"

"Who I fuck ain't none of your business. Move so I can take my ass home. I've had enough of looking at y'all for a day."

"Everyone in this family knows who Dazi is. Why would you fuck her? Can you even imagine how my brother must feel?"

I let out a small laugh. "Look, I suggest you move the fuck around before I hurt your feelings. I don't give a fuck how you or him feels. I barely talk to y'all. Fuck outta here." I quickly walked around her, and just like I expected, she followed behind me.

"You think because you're getting a little bit of money from singing that you can do whatever the hell you want? That's not how things work, Kamari!"

I drew in a deep breath through my nose because Aaliyah was trying me right now. I didn't like arguing in public, and I damn sure didn't like people trying to be all up in my damn business.

"Wasn't you fuckin' brothers, Lee? Didn't you get pregnant and didn't know which one was the damn daddy? Don't say shit to me about loyalty, bruh."

Her face fell because I wasn't supposed to know that information, and I took that as an opportunity to leave. Saint had called an Uber and left after Dazi and Faith did. He was a little hurt that Faith didn't give him the time of day, and I honestly thought it was pretty funny. Saint always thought he could get any woman he wanted, but Faith shut that all the way down.

Once I made it to my car, I called Saint just so I could talk shit to him. He answered on the third ring.

"Fuck you want, nigga?"

"I just called to see how that rejection is tasting. You seemed a little mad when you left earlier."

"Fuck you," He laughed. "She was playing like she didn't want a nigga. I bet if I see her again I'll get her to change her mind."

"Nigga, you said that about getting her to come home with you today, and you see how that went. She already told you she has a type and you're not it."

He smacked his lips. "Man, fuck that. She was lying. Don't no woman want a bum ass nigga. I bet if she knew all the money I was sitting on, things would've gone different."

"Nah, probably not. She doesn't seem like that type of chick. Dazi doesn't either."

"Speaking of Dazi, what the hell did y'all do when y'all snuck off to the bathroom?"

"I did what I said I would do. Had my tongue all up in the pussy. She was loud as hell, too. I'm shocked nobody heard her ass." I could still smell Dazi on my mustache which did nothing but make me want to find her ass and fuck her until she couldn't walk straight.

"Nigga," He laughed. "What it taste like?"

"Exactly what I thought it would. I started thinking about a future with her and the only thing I've done was taste the pussy. I got her number, though."

"Man, tell her to tell her sister to hit a nigga up. Fuck she want me to do? Beg her ass?"

"See, I can't help you with that one. You're gonna have to do that shit on your own. I'm about to head home, though. I'ma hit you up later."

"Aight, bruh." I ended the call without saying anything else.

What I really wanted to do was call Dazi and finish what we started, but I didn't want to seem pressed. All that would have to wait until tomorrow.

*****

The next morning, I woke up to my phone ringing loudly on the dresser, and I let out a low groan. It seemed like I had just closed my eyes, and I was already being woken up.

I opened one eye to look at my phone and saw it was my manager Stacy calling.

"Yeah?" I answered, not hiding the annoyance in my voice.

"Sorry, did I wake you?"

"You know you did. What's up, though?"

"I booked you a performance for next Friday. It's going to be at—"

"Man, you couldn't have waited to tell me this? I could still be sleep right now."

"I know, but I just thought you should know, so it didn't come as a surprise like last time. I'm sorry for waking you. But, since you're awake now, do you want to go get something to eat?"

I let out a low laugh. "Is that the real reason you called, Stacy?"

"No. I called because—"

"I told you I'm not fucking with you like that anymore, ma. Don't call unless it's business related, aight?"

"But Kamari—"

I ended the call not caring about what she was saying. People told me I was crazy for fucking my manager, but I didn't care about any of that.

She was cute, dark-skinned, with long legs, rocked a short haircut, and her lips were full and luscious which is what got my attention in the first place.

I told her I only wanted to fuck, and at first she was cool with it, but of course, she got a taste of this dick and started catching feelings. Something I didn't need her to do.

After ending the call with Stacy, I tried to go back to sleep, but it didn't work. I blew out an aggravated breath just as my stomach growled letting me know it was time to get my ass up and find me something to eat.

What Stacy said about going out to get something to eat didn't sound like a bad idea, I just didn't want to go with her.

Dazi instantly popped in my head, and I remembered we had exchanged numbers yesterday.

Before I could grab my phone, it was ringing again with Cain's name flashing across the screen, and I let out a light laugh before answering it.

"What's up?"

"Aye, I need to talk to you about some shit."

"If it has anything to do with Dazi, ain't nothin' to talk about, my nigga."

"It is about her. I feel like it's a little fucked up that you fucked her at my reception, nigga. What if—"

"Nigga, shut the fuck up with that crying shit," I laughed. "What did you tell me? You said I could have her, right? You shouldn't be worried about anything when it comes to Dazi because you have a whole wife now. I'ma tell you like I told your hoe ass sister. What me and Dazi do is none of your damn business. You couldn't handle her ass anyway, that's why you went back to Dania's boring ass. Say I'm lying."

He was quiet for a second, but I knew his hoe ass hadn't hung up on me.

"None of that shit matters. It's still fucked up that you're even trying to fuck with her. Why would you even want to fuck with her knowing she was my side bitch?"

I laughed again. "Did she know she was the side bitch, bruh? Did she even know about Dania?"

He smacked his lips. "Nah, she didn't, but—"

"But nothing. Dazi ain't your business no more, she's mine. You shouldn't even be speaking her name anymore. Matter of fact, don't call my phone no more talking about her. You been tryin' me lately, and I've been giving you the benefit of the doubt because you family, but in a minute, I'm not gonna care about that shit no more. Don't let this singing shit make you forget who the fuck I am, bruh." I hung up not giving a fuck what he had to say back to that.

There was no reason he should've been calling me this early on some bullshit, anyway.

Quickly, I scrolled through my phone until I found Dazi's number, then clicked on it.

The phone rang three times before she answered.

"Hello?" she said, sounding like she was out of breath.

"What's good? My bad for calling you this early, but I wanted to—"

"This early?" She laughed. "It's almost one o'clock, Kamari."

I smiled to myself hearing her say my name. It reminded me of yesterday when I had her moaning the shit.

"Damn," I laughed. "I thought it was still early. But, shit, you tryna go get something to eat?"

"Mmm," she let out, sounding sexy as hell. "Actually, I am hungry. Let me hop in the shower, then you can send your address so I can be on the way to—"

"Nah, shawty. Don't even disrespect me like that. I can come pick you up. Send me your address."

She let out a small laugh. "Who said I want you to know where I live?"

"You probably want me to come over so we can finish what we started in the bathroom yesterday."

The phone went quiet for a few seconds before she said,

"I do… I can make us something to eat here if—"

"Send your address, ma. Right fucking now."

"Okay," She giggled before ending the call.

Moments later, a text message came through with her address, and I couldn't help the smile that crossed my face as I threw the covers off me and went to get in the shower.

The plan was to take a quick shower, but it didn't happen like that. I had to make sure I had fresh dick for Dazi, so I was in there for a good twenty minutes.

When I was finished with my shower, I brushed my teeth, then I got dressed in some grey joggers and a plain shirt because there was no need to put together an outfit when I was just going over there for one thing.

Well, for two because she said she was gonna cook for a nigga. I was cheesing the entire time as I grabbed my phone and keys and headed out the door.

In my car, I typed Dazi's address into my GPS, then was on my way to her crib. She only lived about twenty minutes from me, and it didn't take me long to get to her place. She lived in a one-story house, and I knew it was hers from her car that was parked in the driveway.

I happily parked behind her car, then got out of mine and made my way to her door where I lifted my hand to knock.

I stood there for about thirty seconds before she finally pulled the door open, wearing nothing but a towel.

"Hey," she said, stepping to the side to let me in. "I didn't think you would get here that fast. I just got out the shower."

She didn't have lime-green hair anymore. It was black, curly as fuck, and in a messy ponytail, making her look good enough to eat.

"It's all good. I guess I did rush my ass over here."

She closed the door and gripped the towel to her body like she was afraid of me seeing her naked.

"Well... you can make yourself at home while I go get dressed, then—"

"Nah," I shook my head. "Ain't no need. You might as well drop that towel."

She stared at me for a moment before she smiled at me, then let her towel hit the floor.

My eyes roamed all over her body, making me instantly brick up, and I motioned for her to come closer.

Seductively, she walked over to me, then stood on her tip-toes to press her lips into mine. Her breath tasted minty, probably from brushing her teeth, and she let her hand travel into my pants and boxers and grabbed my erection.

"Don't be scared of it," I said against her lips, causing her to giggle.

"Boy, bye. I'm waiting for you to show me what you can do with it." She started walking off in what I'm guessing the direction of her room, and I followed right behind her never letting my eyes leave her ass.

She got on the bed and spread her legs apart, showing me her pretty ass pussy, and just like yesterday, I wasted no time putting my mouth on it.

She gripped the back of my head, pushing me further into her while arching her back from the feeling of my tongue swirling around her clit.

"Mmmmm, fuck," she moaned, sounding like music to my ears.

I held her legs open as far as they would go, then slid a finger inside her causing her moans to get louder, and her pussy got wetter and wetter.

I flicked my tongue over her clit over and over making her body shudder each time, and I knew it wouldn't be long before she came.

That wasn't what I wanted, though.

I came up for air and snatched my fingers out of her at the same time and she looked at me like I was crazy.

I just smiled at her as I grabbed a condom from my wallet, ripped it open, and slid it down my shaft. After that, I got on the bed and positioned myself at her entrance then slowly slid into her.

Her mouth fell open, with the moans getting caught in her throat, and I let my hand come up to her neck and gave it a light squeeze.

I ground my hips into her, letting out low moans of my own, while keeping my eyes on her the entire time.

She let the pleasure play out all over her face and I leaned down to stick my tongue in her mouth.

"Kamari," she moaned into my mouth. "I'm gonna cum."

I hadn't even been in the pussy for a good ten minutes yet, and she was already about to cum?

"Fuck you tellin' me for? Cum on this dick."

On my command, her body began to tremble under me, then I felt her gripping my dick.

She was dripping wet, and I had thoughts of taking the condom off... something that's never happened before.

"God damn," I grunted, taking one of her legs and putting it on my shoulder.

Her feet were pretty as hell, but I'd noticed that yesterday in the heels she was wearing.

Not giving it a second thought, I put her toes in my mouth and sucked on them like they were the best thing I'd ever tasted.

I could see the shock written all over her face which let me know she'd been fucking with lame ass niggas. I mean, that shit was obvious since she fucked with Cain's ass.

"Play with that pussy," I demanded, while she bit down on her lip.

Slowly, she slid her hand down to her clit and gently massaged it, making her eyes damn near roll back.

She moaned my name over and over as she came again, and it was getting harder for me to hold my nut back.

"One more time, baby. I need you to cum on this dick one more time."

She started rubbing her clit faster as her legs started shaking, then her whole body, and I was sure the neighbors could hear how loud we both were.

"Kamariii!" she screamed right before she squirted all over me, wetting the bed up in the process.

After seeing that sexy shit, I couldn't hold back any longer.

"Fuckkkk," I let out while filling up the condom.

I collapsed on top of her, trying to catch my breath, and she grabbed my face, pressing her lips to mine again.

"You are dangerous," She said in a small voice. "That's never happened to me before."

"Because you've been fucking with the wrong niggas," I rolled off of her, and my stomach growled, reminding me I was starving. "How about you go cook for a nigga, now?"

She smiled at me before she got off the bed and disappeared out the room.

BE ON THE LOOK OUT FOR THE MILLER SISTERS. THEY'RE COMING SOON.

CONNECT WITH ME:
INSTAGRAM: @writtenbykatcole
JOIN MY FACEBOOK READERS GROUP: KAT COLE'S KITTENS TO STAY UPDATED